For John Mitchell
and Floss

Copyright © 1992 by Kim Lewis

First U.S. edition 1992
First published in Great Britain in 1992 by Walker Books Ltd., London.

ISBN 1-56402-010-X
Library of Congress Catalog Card Number 91-71853
Library of Congress Cataloging-in-Publication information is available.

10 9 8 7 6 5 4 3 2

Printed in Hong Kong

Candlewick Press
2067 Massachusetts Avenue
Cambridge, Massachusetts 02140

Floss

by Kim Lewis

CANDLEWICK PRESS
CAMBRIDGE, MASSACHUSETTS

Floss was a young Border collie who belonged to an old man in a town. She walked with the old man in the streets and loved playing ball with children in the park.

"My son is a farmer," the old man told Floss.

"He has a sheepdog who is too old to work. He needs a young dog to herd sheep on his farm. He could train a Border collie like you."

So Floss and the old man

traveled, away from

the town with

its streets and houses

and children playing ball

in the park.

They came to the

heather-covered hills

of a valley, where nothing

much grew except sheep.

Somewhere in her
memory, Floss knew
about sheep.

Old Nell soon showed
her how to round them up.

The farmer trained her
to run wide and lie down,
to walk on behind,
to shed, and to pen.

She worked very hard
to become a good sheepdog.

But sometimes Floss

woke up at night,

while Nell lay sound asleep.

She remembered

playing with

children and rounding up

balls in the park.

The farmer took Floss
up to the hill one day
to see if she could gather
the sheep on her own.
She was rounding them
up when she heard a sound.
At the edge of the field,
the farmer's children were
playing with a brand-new
black-and-white ball.

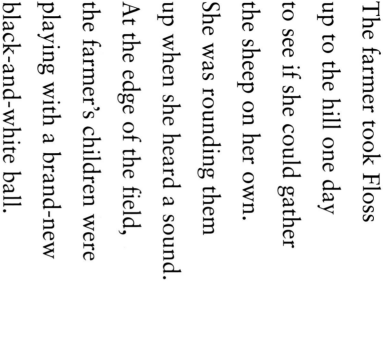

Floss remembered
all about children.
She ran to play with
their ball. She showed
off her best nose kicks,
her best passes. She
did her best springs
in the air.
"Hey, Dad, look at this!"
yelled the children.
"Look at Floss!"
The sheep started
drifting away.

The sheep escaped through the gate and into the yard. There were sheep in the garden and sheep on the road.

"FLOSS! LIE DOWN!"

The farmer's voice was like thunder.

"You are supposed to work on this farm, not play!"

He took Floss back to the doghouse.

Floss lay and worried
about balls and sheep.
She dreamed about
the streets of a town,
the hills of a valley,
children and farmers,
all mixed together,
while Nell had to round
up the straying sheep.

But Nell was too old
to work every day,
and Floss had to learn to
take her place.

She worked so hard
to gather sheep well
that she was too tired
to dream any more.

The farmer was
pleased and ran Floss
in the dog trials.

"She's a good worker now,"
the old man said.

The children still wanted
to play with their ball.

"Hey, Dad," they asked,
"can Old Nell play now?"
But Nell didn't know
about children and play.

"No one can play ball
like Floss," they said.
So the farmer gave it some
thought.

"Go on, then," he whispered
to Floss.
The children kicked the
ball high into the air.

Floss remembered
all about children.

She ran to play with
their ball.

She showed off her
best nose kicks,
her best passes.

She did her best
springs in the air.

And they all played
ball together.